# Aftertaste

# Jennifer Shapcott

# Aftertaste

## Acknowledgements

I would like to thank the following people who gave me advice
on drafts of some of these stories:
Chris, Kyle, Lyndon, Nadia Green, Ann-Mari Jordens,
members of the Ramekins writing group,
Christine McCaffrie, and Rosemary Morley.

*Aftertaste*
ISBN 978 1 74027 764 8


First published in this form 2012
Reprinted 2016

## GINNINDERRA PRESS

PO Box 3461 Port Adelaide 5015
www.ginninderrapress.com.au

# Contents

# Acts of Kindness

It should have been paradise. We were drinking shiraz and sitting on a green lawn sloping down to the river while the sun splashed gold on the eucalyptus trees. But since I'd arrived, Matt and Monica had been squabbling like a pair of monkeys and now Matt was rehashing an ambulance case.

'Poor bastard,' said Matt, refilling his glass. 'After everything that'd happened to him –'

'Charles doesn't know who you're talking about,' Monica cut in.

'Frank was a local character round here,' said Matt, taking a sip of wine. 'First his wife left him –'

'Because she couldn't stand him yacking all day.'

'No, there was more to it than that –'

'Let's face it, he was a bloody interfering old stick. On Sundays he'd pick up our newspaper off the lawn and fling it onto the veranda. No one asked him to. Woke me up every time, made me cranky as hell.'

'You're always cranky.'

'What happened to Frank?' I asked.

'Tell him, Matt. But tell the story straight. Don't go adding bits.'

'I'll tell the story how I want to, or not at all,' Matt replied, glaring at her and lighting a cigarette. He shifted in his deckchair, then leaned back, as if settling in to tell the story. 'Frank was one of those older blokes you see around town, white stubble, old-style work boots and trouser braces. He worked as a foreman at the sawmill, used to sort out blues in the timber yard and help the apprentices. Then he got retrenched and everything changed.'

'What happened?'

'Well, first, his wife Dorothy got fed up with him being round the house all day. Her dream was to travel and take a cruise to Alaska –'

'When all he wanted to do was to ride his bike round town and talk to anybody who'd listen,' interrupted Monica.

'What did he talk about?' I asked.

'Everything. He had an opinion on everything,' said Monica. 'One day he buttonholed me and rabbited on about the granite in the school hall, how it came from the quarry they used for the pylons on the Harbour Bridge. He reckoned I should be teaching more local history at school. When I told him I had to go but I'd Google it, he looked crestfallen, like a dog when you stop throwing a stick.'

'In the end he realised people couldn't be bothered listening to him. That's why he let someone swing an axe at him,' said Matt.

'Someone swung an axe at him?'

'Tell Charles what happened.'

'He set off on his bike one morning –' Matt began.

'Like the local vicar doing his parish rounds.'

'Monica, can I tell this story without you chipping in?'

'OK,' she replied, her eyes narrowing. 'I promise not to interrupt, if you don't go adding bits, like what people are thinking.'

Matt didn't reply but from the fury in his eyes I knew he was going to tell the story exactly the way he wanted.


As soon as Frank walked into the kitchen carrying a pile of wood, Dorothy swore at him for wearing boots in the house. She was tapping at a computer on the table where her friends Maud and Agnes sat drinking tea. Frank noticed that both Dorothy and Maude were wearing pink tracksuits, their bus tour outfits, but Agnes wasn't.

'Would ya like anythin' from the shop, Dot?' he asked, stacking the wood against the stove. 'I thought I'd pop down the road now the weather's cleared.'

Dorothy looked up from the computer with eyes as hard as stones on an empty river bed. 'Fish fingers for tea tonight,' she barked as

Maude spluttered over her tea. 'And don't interrupt again. I'm doing me futures trading.'

'Off to help the local citizens are we, Frank?' asked Agnes.

'Yeah, as only Frank knows how,' sighed Dorothy.

'Why don't you call round at my place some time?' asked Agnes with a wink. 'The lock on my bedroom door's broken.'

A warm breeze brushed against Frank's face as he cycled down the street and tried to erase the memory of Agnes's wink from his mind. He braked when he saw something hanging out of Mrs Applecross's letter box, pulled out a parcel and left it on her front step. He hopped back on his bike and tried to brush away the image of a face at a window and a hand closing the curtains.

Next stop was Norm's servo to help fill up petrol tanks. The old biddies needed to brush up on their driving skills, he reckoned, the way they hit the accelerator as soon as he tapped on the car window for a chat. They'd have to do without him soon. Norm was selling up. Everything would go, the marigolds in the white painted tyres, the bowsers, the workshop, all replaced by a billboard promising a lifestyle for the over-fifties.

He parked his bike outside the leagues club and bounded up the stairs, his eyes slowly adjusting to the dark interior and the carpet with red and green swirls that greeted him along with the jingle jangle of the pokies.

'How ya goin', Frank?' asked Tom, sipping a Scotch and coke.

'Same as yesterday. How are you, Tom, and don't say not bad,' replied Frank, before realising it was no good talking: Tom had switched off, eyes glued to the giant screen watching *Wheel of Fortune*.

Frank downed his beer and got up to leave.

'Ya not goin' now, are ya?' asked Tom. 'They're goin' to announce the raffle for the Honda Accord any minute.'

'They're always announcing somethin'. Every hour of the day from the minute ya walk in. I'd rather gamble on the dish lickers –'

'If ya goin' to put a dollar on the doggies,' interrupted Tom, 'can ya lay a bet on Bold Explosion, Race 5, Maitland?'

'I wasn't but I will.'

After calling in at the TAB, it was off to the boat ramp. Always something going on there – usually a nipper about to be run over by someone forgetting to check the rear-vision mirror. And yesterday the couple driving their boat away with the biminy still up.

The husband had said, 'Thanks, mate. We hadn't forgotten. It's on the checklist,' brandishing a laptop like a shield. 'We always take it down last.'

'Like hell you do,' Frank had thought but propped up for a chat anyway just before they sped away.

Cycling towards the general store, Frank shook his head at the loafers with their noses in newspapers, sipping coffee under black umbrellas outside the shop. Used to be a friendly place but no one bothered to say hello any more. Unbelievable it was; Buddhist statues on the lawn, and the glass and crystal baubles hitting his face when he walked in, and all he wanted was a packet of fish fingers.

The woman with the red hair streaked silver down the middle shook her head. Awaiting deliveries, come back in half an hour and do you mind, that's my mobile ringing. To fill in the time, he wandered down to the river and opened oyster shells with his pocketknife. The breeze had grown stronger and he clutched his hat with one hand as he rode back to the store.

He was cycling across the car park when he caught sight of a man with a ponytail and sunglasses. He was walking with his head down, studying a piece of paper.

'Can I help ya, mate?' asked Frank.

'Nah, I'm right.'

'Where ya going?'

The man looked at him with bloodshot eyes. Fleshy face, lip ring and metal bolt through his nose. 'To a mate's house,' he replied.

Frank peered over his shoulder at the diagram. 'If ya turn ya map around so it's facin' the river –' he said, taking the piece of paper.

'Shit,' yelled the man as the wind blew the paper out of Frank's hand and swept it down the river, where it floated like a white rag out to sea.

'Ya bloody idiot.'

'Can't ya ring ya mate?'

'His phone number was on that piece of paper, ya moron.'

'What's his name?'

'None of ya business.'

'We could drop round to the police station. Dan knows where everyone lives round here. No point in ringin' him, though. Every time I call, a machine comes on.'

'Police station? Forget it, man. I'm out of here.' He began walking away just as a four-wheel drive swung into the car park.

A man in sports trousers and a polo-neck shirt opened the car door and strode towards them carrying a sawn off .22 calibre rifle. He was followed by a man in tracksuit pants and singlet, buffed up like he'd come from the gym.

'You didn't show up, Zac,' said the first man.

'The bloody map blew away because this old geezer stopped me and –'

'Pathetic. Absolutely pathetic. Next you'll tell me he's a plainclothes copper.'

'Rhys, please. I wasn't leaving town. I was just getting away from this stupid old bastard.'

Frank slipped behind a bush as Rhys fired at Zac who dived for cover behind a tree. Zac pulled out a handgun and fired back. When Zac stopped to reload, Rhys raced back to the car and turned into the main road, the car screeching and careering as it hit the gutters. Frank ran to the phone box at the edge of the car park.

'Yeah, I know. Leave a message at the tone. Dan, it's me, Frank. Can ya come down to the car park near the jetty? There's been a bit of trouble. Out-of-towners stirrin' things up. They're still shootin' at each other. Got to skedaddle. Dorothy wants fish fingers for tea tonight.'

From the phone box, Frank watched Zac reload while the man in the tracksuit pants fired from behind a garbage bin. Frank rode off in the opposite direction and let out a sigh of satisfaction. Trouble had come to town and he'd been the first to spot it. He bought a packet of fish fingers and cycled home with a light heart.

The house was dead quiet, curtains closed and the TV switched off.

Then he found the note on the coffee table.

> Me and Maude are going away on a cruise. Agnes says she's happy to keep you company if you get lonely.
> Dorothy

He turned as he heard the back door swing open. He walked slowly down the hall, jumping each time the floorboards creaked. When he pushed open the kitchen door, a man with a ponytail stood in front of him with an axe.

The neighbours heard a scream that chilled their bones.

Matt stopped talking and took a deep breath.

'Did Frank survive?' I asked.

'Yeah.'

'How was he? Did he stay the same? I mean, did he go on helping people?'

'Yeah, he stayed the same. I visited him in hospital and we had a chat in the garden near the river. He was sitting on a bench, sharing his sandwiches with the seagulls.'

'To be honest, I miss the thud of the newspaper on our veranda. It was the only thing that got me going on Sunday mornings –' said Monica.

'Frank didn't get back on his bike in the end,' said Matt, seeing the startled look on my face. 'After he got out of hospital, he walked down to the heads one morning and spotted a couple of young kids struggling in the water. They were caught in the rip, panicking and screaming for help. Frank swam out and brought one girl in then turned round to rescue the other. But she'd been swept out too far – he couldn't reach her. He saw the lifesavers row out but then he got caught in the rip.' Matt paused and lit up a cigarette.

Monica was staring at the river, her grey eyes growing thoughtful while we waited for Matt to continue.

'Frank was calm as he was dragged out to sea,' he said, after a few minutes. 'Maybe the boat would reach him, maybe not, he thought, looking up at the dome of blue sky. He'd saved one kid and raised the alarm for the other. That was enough. The sea could claim him now. Shuffling round a nursing home, shoved in front of daytime soaps, that wasn't going to happen to him. He was going out the way he wanted.' Matt sat back in his chair and sipped his wine.

I stole a look at Monica and noticed her face had softened.

'Poor Frank,' she said quietly before rousing herself and sitting up in her chair. 'You did it again, Matt.'

'What?'

'You added bits to the story. You said what Frank was thinking.'

'Yes – to help Charles understand the story.'

I waited for her retort but she was silent. She was staring at him. The sharpness had returned to her face but when I looked more closely, I thought I saw the glint of admiration in her eyes.

# Green Tea

'I've no idea where Vincent is,' said Luke, cradling the phone between his shoulder and ear as he walked quickly to the front door. 'All I know is his rent's still coming in. Sorry, can't hear you in this rain.'

Kate was walking behind him, clutching her briefcase over her head.

Later, at dinner, she asked him about the call.

He frowned and ran his fingers through his still damp hair, pushing it up into a nest of short black spikes. 'It was the real estate agent for the townhouse.'

'And?'

'He was rabbiting on about an unregistered car that's parked there. The neighbours reckon it belongs to Vincent but he's not answering the door. Are you going to eat the rest of that soup?' he asked, reaching for her bowl.

'Do you think we should go round to the townhouse – make sure that Vincent's all right?'

'No, leave it,' said Luke, scooping up the last of the soup from her bowl. 'Vincent doesn't need running after. Not with his charmed life.'

They were sitting with friends, huddled near a brazier at an outdoor table so Kate could smoke. Luke was sorting out the new waiter who was unfamiliar with their Saturday coffee orders, including the bubbaccino for Clare and Rodney's daughter, Sophie. Kate had just finished telling Clare about the call from the real estate agent.

'I wouldn't worry about Vincent. He's probably gone up north to windsurf,' said Clare, her eyes locked on Sophie, who was crawling after a brown papery leaf blowing along the footpath. 'In any case, he's not your responsibility.'

'I know he's not,' Kate replied, fiddling with a hair clasp and pulling her hair back tightly. She lit up a cigarette and then stubbed it out. 'But Luke and I did share our townhouse with him and –'

'Doesn't mean we're responsible for him now,' interrupted Luke.

'The three of you lived there for a while, didn't you?' queried Rodney.

'Yeah, it helped pay the mortgage,' replied Luke.

'He'll be fine,' Clare declared. 'I've never known anyone like Vincent. Call it serendipity or whatever, it's a bloody miracle the way he climbs out of shit with a grin on his face. Did you hear about the time he hitchhiked from Bath to London? There he is, broke, hungover and staggering down a country lane, when, next thing, a horse gallops by with a man running after it. So Vincent joins the chase and helps capture it. Turns out the owner's a rich horse breeder and Vincent spends the next six months living like a lord in a manor house in Bath.'

'What about the jazz festival in Moruya last year?' said Rodney. 'He turns up at the campsite carrying a six-pack and nothing else. Sophie gets an attack of gastro so we have to turn around and go home. He gets our festival tickets and camping gear – the lot.'

'But things change,' said Luke. 'Heading towards thirty, people have to accept responsibility, they can't just drift along the way he does.'

'I disagree,' laughed Clare. 'I reckon we should put it off for as long as we can.'

'Vincent does that, doesn't he?' said Kate, when she and Luke were walking home. 'When he's not around, people spend their time talking about him.'

'Yeah, I can never understand it. It's as if he's built a reputation out of being disorganised. And everyone admires him for it.'

The real estate agent harangued her as soon as she picked up the receiver. 'Ms Princeton, I've called several times and nothing's been done to remove the unregistered car in front of your townhouse. The neighbours have complained to me again today. Would you mind contacting Mr Harley and asking him to move the car, please?'

'I haven't been able to reach him. I'll talk to his sister Sharon and see if I can find out where he is.'

Two small boys rushed to the door, stared at Kate and scampered away.

'When they heard the doorbell, they thought it might be Vincent,' said Sharon as Kate walked in. 'He often takes them to the park on Sunday arvos.'

'Sharon, I left a message on your answering machine. Do you know where Vincent is?'

'Sorry, missed your message. I've just made a cuppa. Would you like one? Kevin, Kate's here.' She brought three mugs of tea over to a table. 'We haven't heard from Vincent since he finished making this ship for the kids,' she said, pointing to a toy pirate ship standing on a sheet of blue cardboard. 'Do you like it? Check out the toy crocodile underneath the gangplank.'

'Yeah, it looks good,' replied Kate, without glancing at the ship. 'Sharon, no one's heard from Vincent for weeks. I'm really worried about him.'

'I've just realised something. He didn't come round last week and it was the twins' birthday,' said Sharon. She stood up abruptly and grabbed a set of car keys on the coffee table. 'Come on, Kevin. Come on, you kids, we're going to Uncle Vincent's house.'

When they arrived at the townhouse, Kate noticed the letter box was overflowing with letters and junk mail. Her hands shook as she bent down to pick up an empty sake bottle standing near the doorstep. She rattled the bottle and fumbled to catch the key as it fell out.

'Vincent keeps the place neat and tidy, doesn't he?' said Sharon, entering the townhouse and surveying the mugs hanging on hooks and photo magazines stacked in neat piles on the coffee table.

'Yes, he's organised that way,' replied Kate.

She was about to remark how empty the place looked but stopped, recollecting that she and Luke had taken their furniture and decorations with them when they moved out. One picture remained – a black and white photo of eight stepping stones rising above the water in an ornamental pond in Kyoto. She'd taken the photo when Vincent had stayed with her in Japan for a year – before she met Luke. He'd asked her if he could keep it. Luke had agreed before she'd had a chance to answer and joked that it reminded him of a crooked line of stones in a fish pond. Kate's chest had tightened in a sharp band. She didn't want to remember where the stones led to.

The twins raced up the stairs, wriggled under a bed and dragged out toys and games.

'Vincent used to hide things for them to find,' explained Sharon.

'I didn't know he was any good with kids,' replied Kate. She paused at the top of the landing and glanced at the study. 'I'm going to check his computer. I think I still remember his password.'

The computer on the desk was switched off. Kate logged on and scanned Vincent's emails. Nothing exceptional. Just jokes from friends and offers to improve his love life. She flicked over his Internet history.

'What is it?' asked Sharon as she saw Kate frown.

'He's been looking at sites with cheap fares to Kyoto.'

'He mentioned something about going to Japan. Kevin, have you checked our answering machine lately?'

'No, stupid bloody things. I refuse to be a hostage to technology.'

'Might want to come back home with us, Kate. We'll check the machine.'

Back at the house, they replayed a message from Vincent telling Sharon he was going to Japan for a few weeks and adding that he'd left an itinerary in his letter box.

'He's fine,' announced Sharon. 'Sounds as laid-back as ever. End of mystery.'

'Sort of,' replied Kate.

'Why only sort of?'

'Why has he suddenly gone to Japan?'

'I can't answer that one. With Vincent, well, you never know what he's going to do.'

The woman from the embassy told her how to get to the hospital in Kyoto: a tall building opposite a three-tiered pagoda, a short walk from the main railway station. The receptionist at the hospital barely glanced at her when Kate spoke to her in Japanese and asked to see Vincent; perhaps her Japanese was finally indistinguishable from a native speaker or, more likely, she was used to foreigners rescuing friends who'd injured themselves, Kate mused. A nurse took her through a maze of corridors to a single ward and left her at a bed with the curtains closed. Kate coughed and pulled the curtains back.

Vincent hobbled slowly towards her, dragging one leg and meeting her in a clumsy embrace. She took a second look at him. His face was bruised and there was a line of stitches on one side of his head. His blond hair had been trimmed, leaving the curls flattened. She could see his eyes for once – blue, intent and serious. But they soon changed.

'I see you've dressed up to visit me in hospital,' he said, taking in her red jacket and black high heels.

She sat down on the bed and glared at him. 'I came straight from work. I took the first flight I could get and grabbed my passport on the way to the airport. The embassy told Sharon it was an emergency –'

She stopped as two nurses came in to give Vincent an injection and stepped out as they closed the curtains. She heard the nurses tittering as they left, giggling about the tall handsome foreigner.

'What happened? Did you get into some sort of fight?'

'Yeah, I'll tell you about it, later. Right now I want to get out of here.'

At the discharge desk, the nurse gave her a box of medicines and a list of instructions. Her eyes lingered on Vincent as she instructed Kate to ring the hospital if she needed anything.

Kate placed a tray with a teapot and two cups on a low table as Vincent limped across the tatami floor and slid open a paper-screen door. A path of white gravel, glistening from the early morning rain, led to a garden of bamboo and a stone lantern topped with moss. A light breeze stirred in the bamboo, sprinkling raindrops onto the ground.

'Good time to come – the wet season's almost finished, everything's green,' he said.

Kate put down her cup. 'Vincent, have you been in some sort of trouble?'

He moved slowly to the table, took his cup with both hands and looked across at her. 'Yeah. Things sort of got out of control.'

'In Japan? It's the safest place on earth.'

'Yeah, it is.'

'Tell me what happened.'

'Most nights I've been going down to a bar near the canals, you know, the old part of town with the willow trees. I got to know a few locals. They'd shout me drinks and order raw jellyfish or squid – and then watch the look on my face when I tried to eat them. The owner, Yoshio, reckoned I was good for business. He and I talked a lot – hard going with my pidgin Japanese but we managed somehow. He wanted to go to Australia and…' He stopped for a moment and stared out at the garden.

Kate lifted up the teapot and poured, the tea splashing noisily against the sides of the cups.

Vincent took a sip and resumed his story. 'Sometimes a thickset guy with a crew cut and sunglasses came into the bar – looked like something out of yakuza movie. Anyway, one night, he stayed on drinking till midnight and started arguing with Yoshio. All of a sudden, he pulled out a gun and pointed it at him. I tried to knock it out of his hand but he turned on me and I copped a pistol whipping. Then he shot me in the leg. Next thing, I woke up in hospital.'

'Why did you get involved? It was probably a protection racket.'

'I had no choice. He was going to kill Yoshio.'

'But why did you come to Kyoto in the first place without telling anyone?'

Without replying, Vincent picked up the laptop computer lying near to the table and scrolled through a display of photos. 'Do you remember where that is?' he asked, pointing to a photo of blue irises massed near a lake.

'The gardens at Heian Shrine.'

'And this one?'

She stared at a photo of the stepping stones stretched across a pond. 'Yes, you've caught them in a good light.'

'Will we go there tomorrow?'

'Maybe later…sometime…before I leave Japan.'

The furin bell tinkled gently as the afternoon breeze stirred through the bamboo.

'I've got an idea for tonight,' said Vincent. 'Let's catch the train to Uji. We can have sushi and beer by the river and watch the cormorant boats.'

'Are you well enough – after the operation?'

'Yes, if you shout us a taxi to and from the railway station. Sorry, but I've run out of money. Are you well enough? You're hardly eating.'

'That's because I feel nauseous most of the time.'

'You say it like a prisoner facing a death sentence,' he said. 'What is it? What's wrong?'

She shook her head and didn't answer.

In the evening they watched the boats assemble in a cavalcade of lanterns and saw the fisherwomen guide the cormorants on ropes towards the fish. Soon the boats glided down the river and vanished into darkness.

Riding in the taxi back to the inn, Kate started to retch. As soon as they reached their room in the inn, Vincent laid out futon mats and covers on the floor.

'The place where the stepping stones lead to…is that why you came to Kyoto?' she asked, crawling under the futon cover.

'Yes, I wanted to go back – to the place where we scattered the ashes.'

In the still of the night, they heard a woman singing about a mountain village, and the notes of a shakuhachi flute, rising and falling away at the end of the song.

Kate sat up and looked at Vincent without speaking. In her mind she retraced their steps from a journey a few years earlier. The red arch at the entrance, the crowds of tourists, the glare of white gravel in front of the red wooden shrine and walking through the covered bridge over a lake and onwards to reach the pond where the stepping stones lay – huge, round stones that once supported ancient bridges in Kyoto and now formed a path to an island where a small wooden temple stood. In front of the temple, a bed of irises where they'd spread the ashes of their stillborn baby.

'You're shaking,' he said. He put his arm around her. And stayed there, comforting her through the night.

The next morning they visited a nearby temple and walked below cedar trees arching over steps to a wooden pagoda. They lit incense at a large brass urn then walked through the grounds until they reached a grove of maple trees with deep green leaves that filtered out the sunlight. Under the trees stood rows of small white statues, each with a red cloth tied around its neck, some adorned with yellow daisies.

'Statues of Jizō, the Buddhist god who protects children,' said Kate quietly. 'Women pray to him to save the souls of babies they've lost…' Her voice trailed away. She looked across at Vincent. 'Luke doesn't want children.'

He put his camera down. 'Do you?'

'Yes, but not with Luke – not if he doesn't want them.'

'But you do. And you're pregnant. I'm right about that, aren't I?'

She nodded. 'Do you want to go back to Heian Shrine now – to walk across the stepping stones to the island?'

A breeze had sprung up in the gardens of Heian Shrine sending ripples across the pond. Vincent crossed the stones and reached the island where the small wooden shrine stood. Kate paused at the final stepping stone as she watched him walk towards the temple. She couldn't take the last step onto the island. She hadn't found the courage to talk to him.

She caught a glimpse of her shadow moving on the surface of the lake, its shape distorted by the ripples spreading across the water. The breeze stilled and the outline of her shadow grew clearer as the ripples died way. She glanced across at Vincent, who was leaning over a clump of irises, glowing blue and gold in the afternoon sun. As he gently pushed the flowers aside and touched the ground below, she reflected on how carefully he masked his character, projecting a personality to the world that was no more than a veneer.

No words could explain her decision to leave Luke. Some might understand her desire to wrench herself from a marriage bereft of love where children had no place. But few would comprehend her decision to spend her life with a jester who wore a crown of good luck with such careless ease. And no words could explain her love for Vincent: she would have to use stock phrases about people not being as they seemed – clichés and platitudes to help illuminate and unlock his character to the world – if that were possible.

As she slowly took the last step onto the bank of the island, she resolved to ask him the question.


It was a warm spring day. As they waiting for their coffee, Rodney and Clare watched Sophie chase after blossoms falling from the plane trees in pale green flurries.

'I wouldn't have thought being a full-time dad would have appealed to Vincent,' said Clare. 'It's a big thing to step in and father someone else's child.'

'Well, Kate knew that Luke didn't want the baby and it turns out that Vincent loves kids,' Rodney replied. 'I bumped into him and Kate in the mall when I was looking at baby backpacks. He's set up a photo studio in the townhouse. When the baby arrives, he'll work from home.'

'Do you think Kate loves him?'

'Yes. She took me aside when he was buying a pram. She reckons if we'd only opened our eyes, we would have seen the real Vincent, how kind and unselfish he really was.'

'Not just a disorganised piss-head after all.'

Rodney paused and pushed his coffee cup around the table. 'Yeah, that's right. But have you noticed how he always gets out of a mess… how he falls arse backwards into something good – every time.'

# Ghostwriter

Isabella looked down at a page filled with doodles and slammed the notebook shut. She checked her watch. The ceremony was due to start in fifteen minutes; if she slipped out now, no one would notice. She opened the gate and set off through the bush.

Twigs snapped beneath her feet as she followed the path down to the creek. The countryside was dying, dissolving into dust and dirt around her, she thought as she passed dams shrivelled into hollows of cracked earth.

She reached the creek, sat down on a flat-topped rock and stared at the muddy water trickling in front of her. She couldn't write in this desolate land with her mind leaping back to the farm and the streams where platypuses dived. Then she let out a long sigh, remembering that she couldn't write at the farm either, not after her book of short stories had been published. She stood up and brushed the dust off her skirt. It was time to stop making excuses. She would go to the ceremony and pretend she was writing.

As she approached the homestead, she caught sight of the caretaker, Jeffrey standing on the path, leaning on his rake and scratching the grey-white stubble on his chin.

She was about to greet him when he called out to her, 'This is where Joe was murdered.'

'Who was Joe?'

'An old fossicker, used to pan for gold near the creek. People in town reckon he'd buried a chest of gold nuggets at the base of that tree,' he replied, pointing to a fire-blackened tree. 'Couple of blokes come out one night and found him sleeping by the campfire, clutching a bottle of whisky. They started digging near the tree. Joe woke up and they killed him. All for a bag of gold dust.'

'Did they get caught?'

'Nah. The coppers come out, then turned around and rode back to town. After what they seen, they left the body for the crows.'

'What did they see?'

'Reckoned they saw Joe's ghost panning for gold – ' He stopped at the sound of footsteps.

Isabella turned to see his wife Dot walking down the path, her plump shape bulging out of her pinafore. As she drew closer, Isabella noticed her cheeks were flushed and the curls of her hair were sticking to her forehead.

'My goodness, it's hot. Hello, dearie,' she said, nodding towards Isabella. 'Jeffrey, I've been looking for you everywhere. The delivery truck's arrived. I need your help unloading.'

'Wait,' said Isabella as Jeffrey turned to go. 'What happened to the tree?'

'There was a fire a few years ago,' said Dot as Jeffrey opened his mouth to reply. 'We had a writer here who got a set against it. He burnt it down one day because –' She stopped and looked at her watch. 'Shouldn't you be at the awards ceremony, luv? They're expecting you to say a few words, you know, as the writer in residence and all that. Make sure you get a seat near the window. That room heats up like a phone box in summer. Are you all right? You look very pale.'

'I'm fine,' said Isabella. She took a quick glance at the tree and walked to the homestead, her heart beating faster. *Shouldn't you be at the awards ceremony, luv?* replaying in her mind like the torment of an inquisitor.


Isabella took a seat in the glassed-in annex and studied the program, noticing that her name appeared at the start of the proceedings, which were now well underway. She sat back and closed her eyes only stirring when the audience clapped. A writer was talking about character development in novels. Isabella tried to concentrate but slowly her mind began to drift. A burst of laughter from the audience brought her back but after a few more minutes, she stopped listening. She looked out the window and saw a magpie lying on the ground near a water tank where a bougainvillea vine had wrapped itself around the metal like a shawl. The bird lay without moving, its claws facing upwards.

She looked around her and noticed that the man next to her was wiping his brow and the woman next to him was using her program as a fan.

When afternoon tea was announced, a murmur of relief rippled through the audience. Isabella stood up and looked out the window. The magpie had vanished.

She walked out of the annex, enjoying the cool dark hallways of the homestead. A stream of people were bringing out plates of sandwiches and cakes from the kitchen and placing them on a table. The mood lightened as everyone revived. Isabella sat at the back and watched people move round the room, scooping up plates and topping up drinks. A group began reading poems, a bright energy igniting their words, filling her with envy. While everyone put down their plates and clapped, she sat with her hands clasped on her lap.

The audience reassembled in the annex. As the awards ceremony drew to a close, the president of the arts centre signalled Isabella to the podium. Silence filled the room as people turned round to look at her. Moments passed then heads turned away politely as Isabella remained sitting. A woman dispelled the awkwardness by marching to the podium with a bunch of flowers for the president. The audience clapped then stood up, chatting as they drifted outside. Above the clamour, the president invited people to talk to Isabella over drinks.

She escaped to the veranda and leaned against a pillar. When a woman walked towards her with a tray of drinks, Isabella's hand shook as she took a glass and spilled the drink over her dress. She saw a circle of puzzled faces staring at her, turned and ran down the steps.

When Jeffrey had shown her around the cottage, she'd thought it was perfect for writing. A wide jarrah desk looking out on the bush. Nothing to disturb her except parrots squawking in the trees. No television, no DVD; no mobile coverage, just a line to dial out, Jeffrey told her, pointing to a red phone on the wall. Only in an emergency, he warned as he handed over the keys to the cottage.

But after the first morning, she found herself hankering for contact with the outside world. She tried to find a wireless connection, carrying her laptop a few metres away from the cottage in search of a signal where the track sloped upwards; the only faint connection came from near a gum tree where wild bees swarmed around a hive.

On her walks she seldom encountered anyone besides Jeffrey and Dot. They told her they'd stayed on as caretakers after the homestead had been bequeathed to the arts centre.

'We've lived here all our married life. You'd have to put us in a box to get us out,' said Dot, placing a pile of towels on the bed. 'And Jeffrey reckons we're better off helping you young writers than mouldering away in a unit in the city.'

Nothing to disturb her and she still wasn't writing. She was writing even less than on the farm, where she'd blamed Joel for disturbing her when he'd brought in piles of wood or put on a kettle that steamed and hissed. She'd complained so much he'd started to walk around her like a giant on tiptoes.

When she and Joel had first moved to the farm, she'd scribbled early in the morning, in the scraps of time between feeding the animals and working in the vegetable garden. But after her book of stories had been published, she'd stopped writing.

And now, far away in a bush cottage, devoid of distractions, she still couldn't write.

She'd once read that writers revealed their deepest thoughts, their very being, when they wrote. In that case, she concluded, she lacked an inner life; in fact, she lacked any kind of soul at all.

Isabella put her hand up against the sun to watch a pair of blue-tailed honeyeaters darting in and out of bushes. The late afternoon light was flickering on a clump of native orchids and between her fingers she could see the sun sinking behind the hills.

She thought of the sunsets she'd seen with her parents when she'd cycled from the farm to their house on the edge of town and sat with them on the veranda as her father gossiped about things he'd seen that day. As he talked, she imagined the stories she might spin from his tales: the married woman from the next farm; how every Friday she stood near the barn by the river waiting for a battered panel van to turn up. And other incidents; walking past the schoolteacher's house one day, her father had gawked in and seen a birthday party for the teacher's little boy, the one she'd found dead in his cot at three months. The lounge room was filled with balloons to celebrate the day he would have turned one.

Isabella had taken her father's yarns and spun them into short stories. She thought she'd been careful, changing details so no one would recognise themselves. But when a copy of her collection turned up in the local library, people in the valley said she was trampling over their lives. They turned their backs on her in town and banged change down on the counters of shops. Joel said she was imagining it. Then he read the stories and accused her of portraying him as a clumsy yokel who interrupted her writing.

She left the farm soon after, but here, on the other side of the continent, the recollection of cold faces and turned shoulders appeared before her whenever she picked up her pen.


'Nothing but rubbish in her notebook,' announced Jeffrey, heaping sugar into his mug of tea.

'I've told you before not to spy on the writers,' said Dot, passing him a slice of fruit cake.

'She left the notebook open.'

'You still shouldn't have read it. What else did she say?'

'There was stuff about a dead magpie. She's got a thing about birds.

Starts with the kookaburras waking her up at first light when she's drifting off to sleep.'

'She must have trouble sleeping, poor little thing. No wonder she's so pale, wandering about the grounds like Ophelia.'

'She's a slip of a thing. I don't reckon she's a writer.'

'What were you expecting – Ernest Hemingway?'

'I'm not talking about what she looks like. It's her writing. I expected more of a story, not just jottings.'

'You think too much.'

'About what?'

'About everything. We're caretakers here, not literary critics.'


'I can't write at night,' Isabella told Jeffrey when he called by. 'The outside light goes on and off all the time.'

'It's probably out of whack and picking up the possums running round,' said Jeffrey, walking over to the light.

'Sometimes I hear scraping sounds on the roof,' Isabella added.

'Ya know the last writer here reckoned he heard scratching noises.'

'What sort of scratching noises?'

'No idea.'

'The last writer, was that the one that burnt the tree down?'

'That's the one.'

'Do you know why he did it?'

'He couldn't write and he blamed the tree. Reckoned he saw the ghost of old Joe hanging round it.'

'What happened to the writer?'

'Dunno. He shot through as soon as he'd burned the tree down.'


Isabella lay in bed listening to the wind slam against the cottage and shake the window panes. It was when the wind died away that she caught the sound of footsteps on the path.

There was a rap at the window and she heard a whisper. 'I'm here. Can ya see me?'

Her heart pounded as she wrapped the doona cover around her shoulders and walked to the window. The moon had illuminated the garden and the trees were casting shadows across the path. She caught sight of a silhouette moving through the trees, a man holding a pan in his hand, walking towards the creek. She watched and waited. Suddenly the shape turned and walked back towards the cottage.

Fear surged through her body; trembling, she forced herself to crouch down in front of the window sill.

'Listen,' hissed a voice. 'The bloke that told ya all about me, he's out to get ya.'

Her legs shook as she stumbled to the phone on the wall and lifted up the receiver. The line was dead. She ran to the door and opened it. Nothing stirred, not a branch or blade of grass. She shivered then shut the door, bolting it behind her, her heart thumping like a drum in her ears.

A whooshing noise started up from the corner of her room. Slowly it changed into a howl. She pulled the doona over her head and lay awake until the kookaburras began their raucous chorus.

She grabbed her notebook and headed to the creek, where she sat on the flat-topped rock and began writing. Her hand flew across the pages and she soon filled a notebook. For a moment she paused from her scribbling. She shook her head and resumed her writing. She could not afford to worry about what people thought of her stories. She was writing at last.

'Jeffrey, did you fix the fridge in Isabella's room.'

'Nah. Too busy cleaning the gutters.'

'Well, fix it today. It was running like a gale when I went to change the linen.'

'Isabella's left. I saw her heading out the front gate just then.'

'Jeffrey, you haven't been up to your old tricks, have you?'

'What?'

'You know what I mean.'

'She should thank me. She'll get a story out of this.'

# Remembering Lucy

'I can't talk now. I'm working on my acceptance speech,' Hank Salderman snapped at his wife when she knocked on his study door.

'We need to book for our vacation in Vermont –'

'I've just won the highest award for journalism in Illinois and all you can think about is how we're going to spend the money from it.'

Mary-Lou shrugged and withdrew.

Hank sighed and returned to staring at the blank computer screen. Unexpectedly, in recounting his career, questions unrelated to his work had flared up and paralysed his efforts to write: who had loved him, loved him for himself, not because of his success and status? Who had lit his heart with passion? Whom had he loved in his life, if he had ever loved at all?

He decided to read the articles he'd written early in his career in Seoul. He searched through newspaper clippings interwoven with books and cursed Mary-Lou for disturbing them. He paused when he came across a painting – a woodblock print, a snow scene in black and white. He remembered Mary-Lou's words when she'd first found it among his papers.

'This is charming. Why haven't you framed it?'

'Because I don't like it. 'The black and white's too stark.'

'Yes, it's unusual. Most Korean prints are very colourful. Where did it come from?'

'A friend gave it to me in the seventies.'

'Who?'

'A colleague.'

'I'll get it framed, a black wooden frame in non-reflective glass,' Mary-Lou announced.

She'd hung the print over the phone table in the hallway, her eyes resting on it when she made calls to organise dinner parties or bridge games. Sometimes he caught her studying the print – a man and a woman with hooded coats walking towards a thatched cottage, their arms laden with wood, and a child running ahead of them. Snow lay on the ground and on the bare branches of the trees overhanging the path. He wondered if it helped her accept her barrenness – because the child belonged to a place and time in a country she didn't know; but sometimes when she looked at it, she patted the velvet band stretched over her blonde hair and looked away.

When he'd been promoted to deputy editor and they'd moved to another suburb in Chicago, he'd packed the print and hid it in the study of the new house. When she asked where it had gone, he told her he'd put it away because it didn't suit the new furnishings.

As he held the print in his hands, he remembered Lucy's eyes glistening with tears as she'd handed it to him. She'd been listless that morning, lying on the Korean-style mattress on the floor, watching him move around the room as he packed for his trip to Tokyo.

When he signalled he was ready, she rose and passed him the papers.

'What would you do if you got caught?' she asked, handing him three pages of closely written notes.

'I'd say I was just the courier,' he replied, wedging the sheets of paper beneath the lining of his shoe.

'So you'd dob me in?'

'Dob?'

'Inform against me.'

'Yes, I'd have no choice. If I was caught, all the might of the American embassy wouldn't save me from prison.' He'd forced the hardness in his voice to fall away, smiling and adding, 'Relax, it won't happen. By the way, you still haven't told me how you managed to get through the police cordon to do the interview.'

She was silent, her eyes following him as he moved around the room and continued packing. 'It's better you don't know,' she replied at last, studying his face as if it was somehow different, as if his eyes had grown feverish behind his gold-rimmed glasses.

'Hank, come back soon, please,' she whispered.

'I've told you before. I'll be back before fall,' he replied, shoving a handful of books into a suitcase.

He was closing the case when she gave him the woodblock print.

'Damn, I've just finished packing.' He re-opened the suitcase and positioned the print between two books.

When they left the inn to take the path zigzagging down to the railway station, he walked ahead, only turning back when he realised she'd fallen behind. She was staring at the city spread out before them, as if seeing the stone houses and broken-tiled rooftops for the first time.

When she spoke, her voice was strained and unfamiliar. 'Everything is the same and yet everything has changed.'

'Don't talk. When we reach the market, slow down, act like we're tourists browsing the stalls.'

They walked through narrow streets, passing women carrying cooking pots on their heads and children sitting on the steps of houses. At the marketplace Hank pretended to examine wooden trays of kimchi gleaming in the morning. They lingered at the stalls, staring at, but not seeing, dried octopus and fish, and bunches of wild herbs and grasses spread out on the ground.

They walked through a maze of lanes, passing walls plastered with political slogans warning of spies and the threat of invasion by communists from North Korea. Soldiers patrolled the street leading to the railway.

Hank turned when Lucy stumbled. She was about to speak and he shook his head. He read the words frozen on her lips. *Come back soon.*

When he saw the military jeeps outside the station, he told her not to follow but she went with him onto the platform. He didn't look in her direction as the train to Pusan drew away from the platform.

He imagined her reading the article on the front page of the *Tokyo Tribune* the following week – an interview with the opposition leader under house arrest in Seoul. The article appeared under his byline as if he'd conducted the interview. A postscript stated that after two years of high-level investigatory reporting in Korea, he was returning to America to head the newspaper's overseas bureau.

He envisaged her trying to erase the pain of his betrayal by travelling south, staying at an inn deep in the mountains, rising early to catch the first rays of dawn creeping over a statue of a golden Buddha in a cave, as they had once done together. As dawn slipped away and the sky clouded over, she would have walked slowly down the mountain, realising she would never see him again.

He stirred as the grandfather clock in the hall struck midnight. Closing his eyes again, he allowed another memory to surface. He was walking with Lucy through the markets, his arm around her waist. He stopped and kissed her against the wall of a laneway.

Later that day they walked to a temple set high in the mountains, the chant of prayers and the fragrance of incense floating through the air. Mist gathered in the valleys below as a monk led them through a grove of cedar trees.

The conversation with the monk returned like fragments floating in his memory. The monk was talking about the thousand-year-old Buddhist sutras inside the temple when Hank interrupted him.

'I heard a South Korean pilot disobeyed an order to destroy this monastery. Is it true that when he flew over and saw the ancient temple below him, he couldn't bring himself to drop the bombs?'

'Yes,' said the monk, closing his eyes slightly. 'It is true.'

'What happened to him?'

'He was arrested and imprisoned.'

'And when the war finished?'

'He was freed from prison and declared a national hero.'

'Great story.'

'No,' said the monk shaking his head gently. 'No story will outlive the teachings of Buddha or the wars and suffering of this country.'

As they walked through the grounds of the temple, Hank began to dictate into his tape recorder while Lucy walked ahead.

Later, he caught up and put his arm around her. 'What is it now?' he demanded as she pushed him away.

'We come to the most beautiful temple in Korea and all you're thinking about is your newspaper column.'

He released his grip on her arm and they walked down the mountain path in silence, the mist falling like a cold blanket on their skin. Thunder erupted and rain began to fall, swelling streams rushing down the mountainside.

They reached a village at the foot of the mountain and crossed a bridge, the river surging below. Rain fell in horizontal slants, drenching them as they ran towards the railway station. Leaping into the train as it pulled away from the platform, their silence changed to laughter. Lucy shivered and he held her close as they stood watching the rice fields shimmer in rain and sunlight.

Hank sat down at the computer, his hands trembling as he Googled Lucy's name. He scanned the profile on the internet: a journalist for a provincial newspaper in Australia, a moderately successful career but nothing that matched her ambitions and dreams. Something had intervened and waylaid her plans. Had his betrayal shattered her? Had he stolen the scoop that would have launched her career?

The photo on the internet startled him. He didn't see the face of a middle-aged woman; he saw a face from long ago, black curly hair, deep blue eyes, dimpled cheeks and the blush that came at unexpected moments, belying her courage and daring. She was wearing a purple shirt in the photo, the colour of late summer plums, the colour of the long skirts that brushed against him as they wandered together through the streets of Seoul.

The profile on the internet said she had a daughter and gave her age. He stared at the screen as if unable to comprehend the words then typed an email to his newspaper editor suggesting that an Australian journalist he knew with a background in East Asian political reporting should be invited to his award ceremony. He would personally cover the expenses but the offer of the airfare should appear as if it came from the newspaper and not him.

'Googling old lovers is the latest internet craze according to the weekend magazines,' said Lucy, taking a seat at the breakfast table. 'What would you do if a former lover found me on the internet and contacted me?'

'I would forbid you to reply,' John replied, frowning as he looked up from the newspaper.

'What if it was done indirectly, through a third party?'

'I would still forbid you to reply.'

'Why?'

'It would be embarrassing if people found out, if the details ended up on the internet.'

'Embarrassing for whom?'

'For Charlotte.'

'Who's grown up, left home and doesn't care what we do.'

'Embarrassing for me, then. People at work, my clients – they'd laugh at me behind my back.'

'You wouldn't be hurt if I replied?'

'Don't be ridiculous. It's not about being hurt,' he said, rising from the table.

'Once you didn't care what people thought. You were magnanimous,' she thought as he left the room.

Hank took the podium, scanned the faces of the large hall and waited till the applause died down. Familiar faces. It was another delusion on his part, the idea that Lucy might be in the audience.

He scanned the audience again and saw her in the second row, blushing as he caught her eye.

He faltered for a moment then put down his notes and delivered the speech written in his mind. When he neared the end, he paused. He saw the audience exchanging glances and raising eyebrows; he caught a glimpse of Mary-Lou's crumpled and bewildered face in the front row. Everyone was waiting for him to end their puzzlement.

'I never did find out how Lucy got into the house of the opposition leader,' he continued. 'She was fearless, she was audacious – she probably scaled the walls at midnight when the police changed their shift. Maybe she talked her way in. She'd mastered the Korean language and understood the culture. And she had a magnetic quality, a steely determination that the Koreans understood and admired. I'm not surprised she found a way in. I was wrong to betray her. At the time, my editor and I rationalised that publishing the article under my name by saying it was in her best interests and essential for her safety. But an inner voice told me that I'd betrayed her. My message to you tonight is that no scoop should betray the trust of another person – a colleague, a friend, a contact, whoever it may be. I understand that clearly, after thirty years. Until now I've never had the courage to apologise to Lucy. Tonight I want to tell her that I'm sorry and ask her to forgive me.'

The audience began to clap, slowly and unsurely at first. The president of the Press Council walked to the lectern and offered his congratulations to Hank. He observed that the speech reflected the integrity associated with his name and the generosity with which he shared the credit for his stories. He added that he personally knew that Hank had mentored Lucy and presumably she had entrusted him with her notes and asked him to work them into a story. The audience began to clap again, falling into a long and sustained applause.

Hank walked down from the podium as the audience rose from their seats. He left the auditorium, brushing aside colleagues and friends lining up to congratulate him. When he reached the foyer, he caught a glimpse of a woman wearing a purple coat. He followed her as she pushed through the revolving doors and strode towards a taxi rank. He called out to her and she turned, the astonishment still glowing in her face.

# Farewell to the Orchid Lady

The first thing I noticed about Juanita when she walked into a meeting of the Porpoise Bay Orchid Society was that her clothes seemed frozen in the eighties: tight pencil skirt, shoulder pads on a red jacket adorned with gold buttons, like an outfit worn by Michael Jackson doing the moon walk. I quickly surveyed her shoes – black pumps, solid but scuffed around the toes, the sort of thing you see at the bottom of a shoe rack in a charity shop. Her hair was a grey-blonde, cut rather roughly. Yet there was an elegance in her voice when she spoke.

'Thank you, Mr Chairman, for allowing me to introduce myself,' she began, pushing a strand of hair behind her ear. 'I've always wanted to cultivate orchids and I understand that Porpoise Bay has the perfect climate for growing them.'

'Thank you, Juanita. Please sit down. We always ask new members to say a little about themselves, their background, and their experience in growing orchards.'

'There isn't much to say,' she replied, her voice faltering a little. 'I used to grow them years ago but I've lost touch. I guess I'm here to re-learn.'

Later, when we broke for supper, I noticed she hardly drank her coffee and looked ill at ease, as if she wasn't used to socialising. I heard her tell Mario that she didn't have a computer. She seemed surprised when he said she could use the internet at the local library.

I found myself talking about Juanita when I rang my daughter Lara that night.

'Perhaps she's been on an inter-galactic voyage,' mused Lara, 'and she's just been catapulted back.'

'Perhaps she's just re-emerged from an emo cave, like the one where you and your Goth friends used to hang out, in the underpass near the train stop.'

'Where we smoked dope, and you never knew.'

'Well, whatever, I'm glad that stage is over.'

We talked a little more about Juanita's absence from the world before Lara said she had to ring off. My chest tightened when I put the phone down. I'd hoped she'd come down to visit, but she was too busy with her rock band, apparently. I could have done with the company. I'd given up phoning former colleagues in Sydney who said we should do lunch knowing I was reluctant to show my face in the city. Things were tight in investment banking and memories were long. I was as washed up as the shearwaters at Porpoise Bay that plunged into the ocean during their migration south.

I called in at the library and pretended to read the newspapers in the hope of spotting Juanita there. When I saw her tapping at a computer, I approached her from behind. To my surprise, she was reading mathematical formulas and referring to a list of handwritten notes.

'How did you get to be so good at maths?' I asked.

'Oh, Max, you startled me,' she said, colouring a little.

'How did you learn such complicated formulas?'

'I did a maths course…through distance education.'

'What are all the squiggles on the screen?'

'Probability theory.'

'Sounds esoteric. Is it any use?'

'Well, it helps people to understand the odds in life,' she replied, swivelling round on her chair to face me. 'Did you know that each time you toss a coin you have the same chance of getting heads or tails?'

'Only useful on one day of the year really.'

She smiled and her eyes drifted back to the screen.

I left the library feeling that I'd disturbed her in the pursuit of some intense endeavour. I began to study her behaviour at meetings of the orchid society, trying to fathom her character, in particular, which camp she fell into – the traditionalists or the modernisers, as I described them to Lara.

The winds of change had begun to blow through the Porpoise Bay Orchid Society and some members were resisting them. Things came to a head when we discussed plans for the annual orchid show. In previous years Grace and Dulcie had sat at a card table at the entrance and invited people to buy a raffle ticket. I pointed out that we could speed up entry to the show if people bought their raffle ticket elsewhere, or if the person buying the raffle ticket just wrote their mobile number on the ticket butt, instead of waiting for Grace and Dulcie to write out their full name and addresses while the queue grew longer.

'People don't buy raffle tickets just for the prizes,' said Grace. 'They like to have a chat with us while we write their tickets out.'

'Yes, but people coming from Sydney don't expect to spend five minutes waiting to get in,' said Cameron, who, like me, had a good understanding of the way business worked.

'And talking to people is a good way to get new members,' countered Dulcie.

'Just have a look at this, will you,' said Cameron, swiping his iPad to display an application for an online raffle.

'The annual show isn't only about orchid growing,' replied Dulcie. 'People come to meet their friends and catch up on all the news.'

I looked at Juanita to see where she fell on this issue. On seeing my glance, she changed the subject and volunteered to be a marshal at the orchid show. Eyebrows went up on people's faces.

'The thing is, Juanita,' Mario explained gently, 'normally marshals are people of five years standing in the club and they're appointed by a ballot.'

'I'm so sorry. I'm clearly not ready to be a marshal. But I'd be happy to write something about the show for the local newspaper.'

'I'll give you a copy of last year's article,' I said, pleased to have an excuse to visit her.

As discussion moved away from the raffle and to the design of the displays, I realised her intervention had been deliberate.

After the meeting, when we were gathering up our papers, Mario talked about it to me. 'I'm glad Juanita got us off the subject of the raffle,' he began.

'I'm sorry I had to bring it up,' I replied, 'but people expect things to move quickly these days.'

'It's the same as when I tried to sort out the society's book-keeping. Just when we're getting somewhere, we have to start all over again because people dig their heels in. It's like Sisyphus rolling that big rock uphill.'

We walked through the club, passing by rooms with people nursing glasses of beer in their hand, eyes riveted on poker machines as lights flashed around them and machines chimed. It was a relief to step out to a clear evening and see a sky awash with stars.

'It's quiet tonight,' said Mario, glancing down the empty street.

'It's always quiet in this town.'

'There's more to this place than meets the eye,' said Mario with a lilt in his voice that I hadn't heard before. Perhaps he'd shaken off the sadness of his recent years as a widower.

'Ciao, Max,' he said, softly.

'Ciao, Mario,' I replied, as he disappeared into the darkness.

Walking home, I thought about Mario's comments on the bookkeeping fiasco. After managing investment portfolios worth millions of dollars, it had been strange to enter amounts for ten dollars on a page with a sheet of carbon behind it, and then take the book to the bank, where a teller stamped it and chatted to me as if I were a friend. I'd raised the issue of the accounts at an Orchid Society meeting and offered to set up an online payment system. Cameron and several others had agreed but Grace and Dulcie fought against the idea, pointing out that a lot of the society's members didn't have a computer.

Walking through the back streets, I ruminated over whether I was slowly succumbing to the pace of life at Porpoise Bay. My old life seemed to be fading away along with the Italian suits and cashmere jumpers being eaten by moths in my wardrobe.

I turned into the unsealed road that led to my house, still thinking about Juanita, when the hiss and snarl of possums brought me back to earth. I quickened my pace, worried that they'd broken through the fence I'd erected around the vegetable patch. The fence had survived and for a moment my spirits lifted but when I opened the door, my heart sank at the sight of the blank walls in the lounge room and the modular cream suite and glass coffee table I'd leased 'temporarily' because I still hoped to work in Sydney again.

I looked at the clock and glanced over at the brandy bottle on the top shelf of the bookcase, but I went to bed sober – I didn't want to reek of alcohol when I called on Juanita the next day.

The caravan park where Juanita lived overlooked the estuary and consisted of caravans that weren't going anywhere and wooden cabins with closed-in verandas. The plots were too small for backyards so people hung up washing lines or stood clothes racks near the front door. Juanita's house was in Bougainvillea Street. She'd marked it on the map with a comment, 'The streets are actually more like a series of haphazard lanes, but quite charming.'

I walked past a woman in a tracksuit, who seemed oblivious to the fact she had rollers in her hair. She paused from throwing birdseed onto the corrugated roof of her cabin, and gave me a wave as if she knew me. I realised it was Dulcie and waved back.

I opened the gate to Juanita's house and walked down a path bordered by geraniums and Canna lilies. When I reached the front door, I bent down to examine an orchid, a small softwood dendrobium sprouting several new shoots. Beside the orchid stood a freshly planted oleander bush.

Juanita opened the door and ushered me in with a sweep of her arm. She was dressed in blue velvet trousers and a cream jumper with a cowl-neck collar. I noticed the jumper had yellowed with age and there were creases in her trousers as if they'd been folded and put away for a long time. There was a weariness in her eyes and her face was more lined than I'd seen before. She gave me a quick smile and I realised I'd been staring.

'Do you have time for coffee?' she asked.

'Yes, thank you. Then we can go through the press cuttings for your article.'

I sat down on an old brown and orange striped settee and surveyed the kitchen which was as bare as the lounge room. It appeared that either Juanita had few possessions or they were stowed elsewhere, hidden away with the rest of her past.

When she came back with a tray of coffee, it seemed she'd read my thoughts.

'I haven't unpacked much yet,' she said, placing the tray on the pinewood coffee table.

'Where were you last living?'

'In Tasmania,' she replied, hesitating a little. 'Near Risdon Vale.'

'What were you doing there?'

'I'd rather not talk about it – my life went nowhere in those years.'

'I know the feeling.'

'I was just about to take a walk. I've found some native orchids on the path to the lighthouse. After we've had coffee, would you like to see them?'

In the months that followed, Juanita and I walked together several times a week in search of wild orchids.

One day she told me about some orchids she'd found growing in the ruins of an old church. We set off around mid-morning. The birds had fallen silent and the only sounds came from an occasional rustle in the long grass, or the dead casuarina branches knocking against each other in the breeze. We walked until we reached a clearing where the remains of a church stood, a ruin of crumbling red-brick walls dabbed with graffiti.

'We can get through here,' she said, slipping through a gap in the cyclone fence. 'The orchids are just behind the altar.'

I squeezed through the gap and followed her to the sandstone altar.

She pointed to a clump of purple orchids and crouched down in front of them. 'My ex-husband didn't like orchids,' she said. Her voice was trembling and her hands shook as she reached out to touch the dark edges of the petals. 'He thought they were poisonous.'

'He didn't know much about orchids then.'

'No. He didn't know much about plants at all. He didn't realise that some plants look harmless but aren't, like oleanders or foxgloves.'

'Or daffodils.'

'But with daffodils, not all parts are poisonous.' Her voice faltered and she leaned against the altar.

'Is anything wrong?' I asked.

'I was just thinking about my husband…'

We were standing wedged between the altar and the crumbling walls of the church enclosed by the fence. I had a sense of foreboding, as if she was about to tell me something I might not want to hear. I suggested we walk up to the ridge, along the cliff path.

'There's a spot where the ridge flattens out. This time of year, we might see some humpback whales.'

Her voice had regained its composure. 'I know the spot. It's like a viewing platform.'

We were walking towards the edge of the point, where the path narrowed into a ridge, when she asked me how long I'd been growing orchids.

'I started after I broke up with my first wife,' I replied. 'Growing them helped keep me sane in between divorces and losing my job, so I know a fair bit about cultivating them.'

She laughed a little. 'It strikes me you don't belong in Porpoise Bay any more than I do.'

I decided to tell her a short version of the truth. 'I used to work for an investment company. I advised clients on how to invest their retirement savings. I was making a mint. Then the global financial crisis struck. My clients lost a lot of money.'

'How much?'

'Almost everything they owned.'

'No one knew the stock market was going to collapse like that.'

'No, but the way we worked with leveraged investments, we knew they weren't sustainable. It was only a matter of time before we crashed.'

I glanced across at her, anticipating her disapproval but she showed none. I wondered if she understood the scale of my destruction of people's lives. Perhaps something in her own past made her reluctant to judge me.

'So you've gone from being an investment banker to president of an orchid society?' she asked.

'With a step in between. Shortly after I'd joined, Mario approached me to stand as treasurer of the society, obviously unaware that I'd lost several millions of dollars of other people's money.'

'You don't miss your old life?'

'Less and less as time goes by. To be honest, managing the society and caring for orchids in black plastic pots in my backyard is enough for me these days. I know I should move on, but I'm not ready to, not yet anyway.'

I looked out over the expanse of ocean, wondering how to explain that I was starting to recover, to regain my zest for life, especially with the help of her friendship. But she had begun to move away, inching along the ridge like someone walking a plank.

'Come back, Juanita. You're too close to the edge.'

'It's not dangerous. I can see a clump of casuarinas on the ledge below.'

'Which is a fifty metre drop. For God's sake, come back.'

She was standing with her body leaning out towards the ocean, like a figurehead on the prow of a ship. She seemed exhilarated. It took me some time to get her to move away from the edge.

'So she's a risk taker,' said Lara.

'It seems like it.' I spoke calmly, belying the anger I'd felt during the silent walk back to Juanita's house and the curt farewell I'd exchanged with her. At the moment we'd become closer, she'd cut me off.

'A risk taker and…possibly a poisoner?'

'What makes you say that?' I asked. I should have rejected the idea but I was thirsting for some sort of revenge, and maligning Juanita seemed a fair starting point.

'It all adds up. She lived near Risdon Vale – Risdon Prison, if the truth be known. She knows a lot about poisons. I bet she tried to poison someone, probably her ex-husband. That's why she's been away from the world.'

'She's been locked away?'

'Exactly. Look, I've got a colleague at work, Daniel, a lawyer who used to do forensic research for a law firm. He knows how to trawl through court cases and newspaper records. I'll send you anything we find out.'

Lara seldom bothered to mention the names of her friends so when she did, it always meant something.

'I haven't heard of Daniel before. How long have you known him?'

'About a year.'

'Why would he help you like this? He must be a good friend.'

'He is. I have to go now, Dad.'

When I put the phone down, I wondered whether I should worry about the idea of Daniel but decided to put him out of mind.

Lara rang a few days later. Daniel had unearthed information about a woman in Hobart who'd poisoned her husband by mixing oleander sap in his food, gradually increasing the dose over a number of months. The court report from the eighties said that her husband, a strong healthy man who'd worked in an abattoir, had gradually weakened and died. The woman had married him a few years earlier and was due to inherit his house and savings. Lara sent me a newspaper clipping about the case and wrote at the top of the news clipping, Who knows, she might have changed her name. Any resemblance?

I scrutinised the photo. I told Lara the truth – there was a faint likeness, not in the hair which was permed tightly, but something about the eyes and the shape of the mouth with its enigmatic smile.

The next time I visited her, I noticed that the oleander plant was shooting up and the first buds had begun to appear. A week later as I entered the house, I noticed that the bush had been snipped.

'Oleanders look good in a vase, don't they?' said Juanita, gesturing towards the coffee table. As she poured coffee, she told me of her plans to make biscuits for the orchid show.

I had a sudden vision of her taking the oleander stems from the vase, placing them in a saucepan of boiling water and adding the water to the biscuit mix. I told her we had enough cakes and biscuits.

'It wasn't going to be a large basket,' said Juanita. 'Just a small offering – I thought I'd wrap the biscuits in cellophane and a large red ribbon. Besides, I've already promised Grace and Dulcie that I'd bring biscuits.'

On the morning of the orchid show, Juanita placed the basket of biscuits on a table. I kept an eye on who ate them, just in case, but everyone bustled around happily and there were no reports of illness in the town that night.

A few weeks later, I told Lara about how Juanita had brought a plate of muffins for supper at the orchid society.

'When she passed the plate around, I took one.'

'Wasn't that a bit risky?'

'I've decided she's OK. I've asked her to consider standing as treasurer at the annual general meeting next week. I can't see any reason not to trust her.'

'I suppose not.'

A few weeks later, after Juanita had been elected treasurer, I called on her. I stepped back when Mario opened the door in a crimson dressing gown.

'Max, I'm so sorry,' Juanita called from the kitchen. 'I didn't expect you this early.'

'I didn't mean to intrude,' I replied, my voice hollowing in my throat.

'You're not intruding,' said Mario. 'You're always welcome.'

'I can't stay. I came by with some cheques for Juanita to sign.'

They urged me to stay but I excused myself, saying I had paperwork waiting at home. They stood at the door and waved me off the premises as if they were standing on the steps of a harbour mansion.

That night I rang Lara and told her about Mario. Without thinking about it, I found myself turning my sense of betrayal into a joke about poisoning. 'Mario's a wealthy widower. He seems besotted with her. Should I warn him?'

'No, not yet,' said Lara. 'Just keep an eye on him, especially if he loses weight.'

When Lara asked me about Mario a few months later, I told her that I'd been wrong. It was time to end the game.

'Mario's growing rounder and happier by the day. He's flourishing.'

'I still think there's something weird about Juanita,' said Lara.

'So do I. But so far, I've been wrong about her.'

The words helped me to hide my despair: Mario and Juanita had become a couple and cut me out of their lives.

I left Porpoise Bay after Lara rang me to tell me there was an opening for a part-time bookkeeper at her work, a welfare rights organisation.

'I told them about your job as an investment banker but they weren't interested in that. It was only when I said you'd been treasurer and then chairman of a community organisation at Porpoise Bay that they agreed to consider you.'

'It's a step down from my previous job.'

'Well, you don't have to take it, Dad. But, it would help me out.'

'How's that?'

'I'm pregnant. On your days off, you could look after the baby, when Daniel and I are at work.'

It was the best news I'd heard for years. As for the job, it wasn't the sort of work I'd envisaged but I was ready to leave Porpoise Bay and return to Sydney so I took the position.

Several years later. I received a letter from Mario.

Dear Max,

I wanted to let you know that Juanita died last month.

She hadn't been well for some time. I think events in her past took their toll more than any of us realised.

When I first met her, I sensed there was something troubling her. She was good at disguising her past but gradually I put the story together.

Juanita came to Porpoise Bay with a new name, to make a fresh start, determined to pay back the money she'd stolen from her work, borrowed from family and friends, and gambled away. Her husband had divorced her. Family and friends had rejected her.

You probably noticed that she almost never bought anything new. Even her clothes belonged to her old life before she went to prison. The only money she spent apart from food was for the Orchid Society. The first new thing she had at Porpoise Bay was the oleander plant I gave her.

She was petrified that people would find out about her past. Even worse, she lived with the fear that her addiction would claim her once more.

Every time she walked past the pokies at the club, she felt close to temptation. She'd had counselling in prison but still struggled. She followed the advice of a fellow prisoner: find another passion, like keeping chooks or growing roses. If you find yourself tempted, tell yourself it's just an idea, and you won't actually do it.

Juanita learned that reading about the mathematics of gambling and treating it as a theoretical exercise helped her to stop thinking about actually gambling. It's strange but she said it stopped her from actually doing it.

Cultivating orchids helped fill a big gap in her life. She told me that the way our orchid society welcomed her and trusted her was really important. It helped her to overcome her addiction.

She mourned when you left Porpoise Bay, especially because she sensed our relationship had come between you and her. But she remained grateful for the way you'd accepted her. She said that because you'd accepted her, the rest of the Orchid Society accepted her, and trusted her.

I hope all goes well for you in Sydney.
Best regards to Lara and her family.
Ciao,

    Mario

I put the letter down and held my head in my hands. Since I'd left Porpoise Bay, I hadn't been in touch with anyone there. I hadn't even replied to the Christmas cards that Juanita and Mario had sent me since I'd left.

The Porpoise Bay Orchid Society had helped both Juanita and me to reclaim our lives. She and Mario had given me friendship then pushed me out, forcing me to find my way without them.

A vision of the sea shimmering through dappled-bark gum trees came back to me and once again I walked with Juanita on the cliff tops of Porpoise Bay in search of wild orchids.

# Aftertaste

Clarissa's dream of driving a sports car almost vanished when her son announced he was taking her off the road and selling her Mazda 323.

'You're a hazard to other drivers, Mum,' Richard said soon after he arrived in Canberra. 'I heard that you crashed near Julia's farm the other day.'

'It's the last turn on the road. It's difficult to judge –'

'I'm not arguing. I'm advertising the Mazda on-line, right now,' he replied, tapping on his iPad.

A few moments later, he strode out of the house and climbed into a taxi, his coat over one shoulder, as if he'd just dashed across a street in Manhattan, thought Clarissa. She couldn't wait till he went back there.

Despite Richard's decree, she still dreamed of driving a sports car down the mountain road to Julia's farm, sweeping past gullies laced with ferns and traces of mist drifting up from the valley below.

When Richard rang to say he'd found a buyer for her car, she invited him and his fiancée, Ellen, to a family lunch the following Sunday.

Richard's scorn sizzled down the phone line. 'You've invited Scully? Julia's manservant?'

'He's not her manservant. He manages her farm.'

'Her valet, then, her bogan valet. Her hired help for the hobby farm.'

'Actually, these days he's her boyfriend. Her sort of partner, she tells people.'

'I don't believe it. When did that happen?'

'They've been a couple for about a year now.'

'I hope she doesn't ride pillion on his clapped-out motorbike. Has he still got it?'

'His vintage Triumph? Yes.'

'He'll wipe himself out one day – and take someone with him.'

'He rides very carefully. Anyway, I'll see you on Sunday. It's Anzac Day, by the way.'

'That won't mean anything to Ellen.'

'No, I wish…'

'You wish what?'

'I wish the wedding was in Australia.'

'Ellen's folks wanted the wedding in New York. There was no other choice.'

'Apparently not,' replied Clarissa, slamming the receiver down.

'Richard doesn't want me at the wedding – that's why it's in New York,' Clarissa said out loud as she climbed a stepladder and delved into the shelves of the pantry in search of ingredients.

She paused as she caught sight of her reflection in a shiny metal canister showing her hair sticking out in peaks of white and her blue eyes blazing like a madwoman. She looked away, reached for a tin of golden syrup, slipped off the ladder and crashed to the floor, where she sat, rubbing her sore knee, and ruminating on Richard. Since John's death, her son's resentment of her had simmered like a pressure cooker. Sorting out John's papers, he'd found his school reports, and she'd been careless enough to mention that she couldn't remember any of them. He'd turned on her, accusing her of being absent during his childhood. A disorganised daydreamer, he'd called her, recalling the times she'd forgotten to pick him up from school because she'd been so absorbed reading novels. Now, back from New York for a brief visit, he poked around the house, and drew attention to the unopened letters and unwashed dishes on the kitchen bench.

She dragged herself up and assembled the ingredients. As she stirred the mixture, she flicked away the lengthening ash on her cigarette and began to plan the lunch – a barbecue on the patio, chrysanthemums in a vase on the outdoor table. Ellen would love Canberra this time of year, with the poplars near the lake soaring against a cloudless sky.

'Nice set of wheels, Richard,' said Scully, hooking his thumbs into the back pockets of his jeans as he walked around the car.

'I ordered it specially from the hire car company. I only picked it up this morning,' replied Richard. 'Mum, say hello to Ellen. Are we going inside or what?'

Clarissa stood transfixed, staring at the car – a black hard-top convertible with leather seats and a leather steering wheel. She took a deep breath, stubbed out her cigarette on the letter box and walked inside.

When she heard Richard swearing, Clarissa left the kitchen, crept out to the patio and peered through the trellis.

'Don't eat the biscuits,' said Richard, spitting into a bush. 'They taste weird.'

'What sort of cookies are they?' asked Ellen, staring at the plate of biscuits.

'Anzac biscuits,' replied Julia, wrinkling her nose as she examined one.

'I don't understand,' said Ellen, turning towards Scully.

'During the First World War, women in Australia cooked biscuits for the diggers in the trenches. They were called Anzac biscuits to commemorate the diggers' landing at Gallipoli,' he replied.

'What were they made of?' asked Ellen.

'Flour, golden syrup, oats with butter and coconut were the main ingredients. But no eggs. You couldn't get them during the war because so many farmers had joined up.' He pushed his fingers through his dark curls, his eyes shining with excitement.

Like a little boy at show and tell, thought Clarissa, staring through the vines. Scully was interested in everything, John used to say – a cross between an English parson exploring the countryside with a butterfly net and Mellors, the gamekeeper in *Lady Chatterley's Lover*, the way he strode through the bush with a rifle slung over his shoulder. 'But not taciturn like Mellors,' she said to John.

'And without Lady Chatterley's husband in the background,' John had added, because the only thing Julia was married to was her job.

She roused herself to stop the conversations with John replaying in her mind.

'Golden syrup?' Ellen was asking.

'It's like maple syrup –' Scully began.

'I don't know why Mum makes Anzac biscuits,' interrupted Richard, spilling his wine as he thumped his glass down on the table. 'She only started cooking them after Dad died.'

'She told me John was a nasho,' said Scully. 'She said he opposed the war in Vietnam but reckoned if his country asked him to serve, he should. Making the biscuits is a way of honouring your father, I suppose,' said Scully.

'That's nice,' said Ellen, curling a strand of honey-blonde hair round a finger. 'Real nice. And what are these cakes, Scully?'

'Lamingtons. Taste one,' replied Scully, holding one towards her.

Ellen bent forward, her cleavage deepening. Richard exhaled sharply as she pushed her tongue towards the lamington and began to eat from Scully's hand. She smiled and licked away the crumbs of coconut that had gathered round the corners of her mouth. Scully passed her a napkin. When she hesitated, he leaned over, took the napkin and dabbed around her mouth.

'I think I'd like some more,' said Ellen.

'No, you'll be sick,' said Richard. 'I'm getting rid of them.'

'Isn't it a little strange to have cookies before a barbecue?' asked Ellen.

'Maybe,' replied Scully. 'But we think that having salad like a separate course is strange. I've heard you do that in America.'

'Only in fancy restaurants,' smiled Ellen, her eyes lingering on Scully's.

'Mum's losing it. We need to sort something out,' said Richard, pouring himself more wine.

'There's nothing to worry about, anyway. She's just absent-minded,' said Julia, frowning as Scully poured a glass of wine and passed it to Ellen.

'Where is she now, by the way?' asked Richard.

'I don't know. It's gone quiet inside. Maybe you should check on her.'

Clarissa crept back to the kitchen and was clattering saucepans when Richard walked in.

'The Anzac biscuits tasted like you'd scrubbed the cake-tin with Ajax and forgot to rinse it,' said Richard, dropping a pile of plates into the sink.

'I'm so sorry, dear.'

'And can you lay off smoking in front of Ellen? It was disgusting the way you greeted her with a cigarette stuck to your lips,' he said, slamming the door on the way out.

Clarissa took a bite from a biscuit and shook her head. She must have put too much bicarbonate of soda in the mixture, she'd been so distracted planning the lunch. But it was only a suggestion of bitterness, not enough to carry on about.

She heard Richard outside yelling for methylated spirits to light the barbecue. She peered into the cupboard under the sink, pausing for a moment, wondering whether he would notice the colour of the liquid.

He didn't look at the bottle when she passed it to him. She returned to the patio a few minutes later with a jug of water, just in time in time to hear Richard cursing.

'Bloody hell, Mum,' yelled Richard, staggering back as a cloud of oily smoke filled the air. 'I asked for a bottle of methylated spirits, not turps.'

'Sorry. The bottles look the same.'

'No, they don't. The turps bottle is brown and the metho bottle's clear.'

'Well, you didn't look then. Anyway, no harm done.'

'Yes, there is. The chicken smells like it's been through a grease and oil change. I hope the water jug isn't full of metho.'

'Serves you right, Richard. I told you to let Scully light the barbecue,' said Julia.

After lunch, snatches of conversation drifted through the window as Clarissa dozed in the sun room.

'The stink clings to everything.'

'I can't believe you're still going on about it, Richard,' said Julia. 'Get over it, will you?'

'I can't get over it. My mouth feels like I've drunk insect spray.'

'Think of the turps as the perfect marinade for a barbecue. It sears the meat and repels the flies,' said Scully.

'What a lunch,' said Julia, shaking her head. 'Make me a coffee, Scully. I need to drown out the taste of turps.'

'I'll have a coffee too,' said Richard.

'Ellen, what can I brew for you?' asked Scully.

'Spiced chai tea, please.'

'I'll check but I doubt I'll find any. Clarissa drinks Darjeeling. Would you like to try some?'

Clarissa imagined the smile accompanying the flash of Ellen's white teeth as she nodded in reply, and her eyes resting on Scully's backside as he walked to the house.

Clarissa took a breath. The conversation had shifted, jolting her.

'Julia, I want you to book Mum in for an assessment,' said Richard.

'What sort of assessment?'

'Tests for dementia – memory, mental acuity, capacity to plan.'

'Tests where they ask you the date and the name of the prime minister? She'd pass easily. She reads two newspapers a day.'

'I wouldn't pass. I can hardly plan my clothes for the next day,' giggled Ellen.

'It's not a laughing matter,' said Richard. 'Mum needs help. She's losing it.'

'Richard, there's nothing wrong with Mum,' Julia replied. 'She might have the occasional memory lapse but she's still got her wits together. She and Scully talk for hours.'

'I'm surprised they have so much in common.'

'Well, for a start, they're both crazy about cars. You shouldn't have sold Mum's Mazda, by the way. She'll just go out and buy something else, and it'll probably be faster.'

'Apparently I'm the only responsible person in this family. She got three speeding fines last year. She's like Toad in *The Wind in the Willows*. You could put her in prison and she'd escape dressed as a washerwoman and steal a car.'

'That's a ridiculous thing to say, Richard. Mum would never steal a car.'

Clarissa heard the backdoor swing open. Scully, carrying a tray with tea and coffee. It was time to strike back. As she walked to the back door, she picked up Richard's car keys from the coffee table and slipped them into the pocket of her apron. 'How's your photography going, Scully?' she asked, sitting down at the outdoor table.

'You're a photographer?' asked Ellen.

'Yeah, I do a bit.'

'When he's not looking after me,' said Julia, placing a hand on Scully's arm.

'Do you ever take studio photos?' asked Ellen.

'Not really – I like to take photos of people that are, you know, sort of natural.'

'Some photographers say my face is difficult to capture.'

Julia's hand slid away as Scully rested his elbows on the table and studied Ellen's face.

'What would you focus on?' asked Ellen.

'The eyes.'

'Yeah, people say the green-grey colour goes well with my dark eyebrows, but my nose lets me down. It's such an ornery ski-jump nose.'

'I don't reckon it's ordinary,' Scully replied, gazing at Ellen's face. 'It's almost queenly, like the rest of you.'

Richard's face reddened and Julia's eyes rounded in disbelief.

We're watching the first steps in a dance of flirtation, thought Clarissa. And we're mesmerised. She'd asked Scully about his photography to irritate Richard. She hadn't expected the frisson of sexual excitement that followed.

'So how would you take a photo of me?' asked Ellen.

'For God's sake,' erupted Richard. 'I've had enough. Ellen, we're going home.'

'Wait. Ellen, who are the photographers you mentioned a minute ago?' asked Julia. Her eyes hardened like an interrogator preparing for an inquisition.

'Oh, I do a little modelling here and there.'

'Really? Richard said you worked in marketing.'

'I work in a jeweller's shop.'

'A jeweller's shop? How strange that Richard never mentioned that you were worked in a shop.'

'So what?' interrupted Richard. 'I don't tell you everything that Ellen does. Unlike the way you rave on about Scully.'

Scully gathered up the coffee cups, his hands shaking as he put them on the tray. 'You're talking about Ellen and me as if we're not here,' he said, picking up the tray.

'Mum, do you know where my car keys are?' asked Richard, a short time later. 'I left them on the coffee table in the sun room.'

'I've no idea, dear.'

'Scully, I need you to drop me at the car hire company so I can pick up another set of keys.'

'Not likely on Anzac Day,' said Scully, 'I'll take you back to the hotel. You can catch a taxi to the hire place tomorrow.'

After they'd left, Clarissa lingered in the driveway, staring at the convertible, which gleamed like a black beetle in the afternoon sun.

As she stacked the dishes, she tried to define the point at which the lunch had gone off the rails. Probably when she'd asked Scully about his photography, she realised. She'd done it to annoy Richard because he hated Scully getting any attention. Revenge always seemed to backfire in her hands.

She imagined Scully and Julia driving home in silence, and later Scully, pretending nothing was wrong, sitting down to watch the Anzac Day football match, then Julia turning on him and accused him of flirting with Ellen. Scully would stand up, put his arms around her and calmly tell her she was imagining it, and that he loved her. But Julia would ignore him, her voice hardening as she told Scully he had better move on and find 'another position'.

Clarissa walked out to the patio, lit a cigarette and fingered the car keys in her apron pocket. She shivered as the air around her cooled and rain began to fall. A few moments later, she set off in the black convertible for Julia's farm.


Richard walked out of the viewing room of the funeral parlour. The mourners pressed around him with words of sympathy that he accepted with a slight incline of his head.

'She always had trouble with the last turn on the road near Diana's farm,' he said to the group. 'But she shouldn't have been driving at all, much less a car she was unfamiliar with.'

'She was perfectly capable of driving that car.' Scully was standing at the doorway, his motorbike helmet under his arm. His jacket was zipped up as if he'd just arrived and wasn't staying. 'She knew what she was doing. There was nothing wrong with her driving that night,' he continued.

'How do you know that?' asked Richard.

'Because I was travelling in the opposite direction. She swerved to avoid me. I'd taken the bend too wide.'

He strode into the viewing room, kissed the body in the coffin, then walked out of the funeral parlour and passed through an archway into the bright cloudless day outside.

# Open House

Rob and Lisa walked back from the hospital through the park, pushing against a wind. Leaves spun across their faces and swirled along the path.

'The trees in the park aren't even swaying now,' Lisa said later, standing at the window of the apartment.

'Have I been there?' asked Rob.

'Yes, this morning. You had a good time.

'Isn't that nice, Rob?' trilled Claudia, entering the room. 'Enjoy it one moment, relive it the next – ' She broke off as her phone rang and stepped out onto the balcony.

'Thank you for letting us stay here,' said Lisa when Claudia returned.

'It was the least I could do. Stay as long as you like. I won't be selling until the real estate market improves.'

'We'll look for somewhere else soon.'

'You should have told me earlier that Rob was ill, not waited till I ran into you in Collins Street. I was your best friend at school, after all – along with Belinda.'

'Actually, I was going to ring her and ask if we could stay at her house for a while. It would give you a break.'

'I doubt if she'd be able to help. She's starting up a new café, and she's not good around invalids.' She paused and added, as if Rob had just left the room, 'He seems content anyway.'

'Yes, except when he realises what he's lost.'

'He understands that they can't treat the tumour?'

'Yes, he knows his sight will deteriorate.'

'How terrible. He was such a great reader.'

'He's still the same person,' said Lisa, stiffening.

'Of course,' replied Claudia. She turned to Rob, who was watching a wildlife program, and said in a loud voice, 'You can go to the park every day while you stay here.'

'Can Almond come too?'

'You don't mind us bringing Almond down from the farm, Claudia?'

'Of course not,' she replied, frowning as she pulled a strand of blonde hair into a clip at the back of her head.

'And Ricky?' asked Rob.

'We'll bring him down later,' Lisa replied. 'When we find somewhere to live.'

'I can show you some houses for sale around here, if you like,' said Claudia, passing her a brochure of a two-storeyed mansion that reminded Lisa of a cruise ship the way its lights shone and its giant curved windows glowed against the city sky. 'It's not in your price range but it'd be interesting to visit.'

'Thank you, but I don't want to traipse around a McMansion.'

'It's not a McMansion. It's excellent quality and it's across the road from the park so we can go for a walk there afterwards. It'll be fun, I promise you.'


'I'm sorry, sir, you can't bring the dog inside,' said the real estate agent at the entrance.

'Don't worry, Rob, we'll tie her up to that skinny birch tree over there,' said Lisa. 'Do you have a bowl?' she asked the agent.

'No, madam. I'm sorry but this is a display house. It's not equipped.'

'A great big house like this and you don't even have a bowl?'

People walking into the house turned at the sharpness of her voice.

Claudia shrugged and smiled at the agent, who fingered the collar of his shirt.

Lisa walked to their rust-pocked ute parked in the street and returned with a bowl which she set down in front of the red-cloud kelpie.

A woman and a young girl walking up the driveway stopped as Lisa poured water into the bowl.

'What's her name?' asked the girl.

'Almond,' replied Rob.

'Is that because she's got almond-shaped eyes?'

'No, it's because when she was a puppy she loved almonds. She used to break them open with her jaws.'

'He remembers that,' said Claudia.

'He remembers last year and the years before. It's yesterday that's slipped away,' whispered Lisa.

As they walked back to the house, Lisa smiled at Claudia struggling in high heels that sank into the lawn, but when they reached the entrance, the agent looked down at her work boots and she found herself wishing she'd changed them. She watched Claudia's red manicured nails move quickly across the page of a book that the agent had asked her to sign. When Claudia passed the book over, she shrugged and put her hands in the pockets of her jacket.

'Why do the agents make us sign the book?' she asked, surveying the empty foyer of white tiles. 'It's not as if there's anything to nick.'

'It's so they can ring people about other properties. I might register for the auction – this is the only house for sale that faces the park. It'll be fun to watch the bidding.'

'Reminds me of Grandad's house,' muttered Rob, taking off his stockman's hat and gazing up at a chandelier. 'Lit with a hundred candles.'

'Not exactly an energy-saving device,' said Lisa, staring at the lights cascading from the ceiling.

'It'd only be switched on for entertaining,' said Claudia.

'The whole house looks like it's only for entertaining,' Lisa replied.

Entering a kitchen of black tiles and marble bench tops, Claudia drew their attention to a second kitchen tucked away at the end for caterers. 'The main kitchen's for everyday use because it's got a microwave and easy-to-clean hotplates,' she explained.

Upstairs they entered a bedroom overlooking the park, where pin oaks glowed in a line of russet.

'I can see trees from here,' said Rob, sitting down on the bed.

'And have you noticed the telly on the wall?' Claudia asked

'Yeah, that's a whopper of a screen.'

'There's even one in here,' called Claudia, entering the en suite. 'The bathroom fittings are superb, by the way.'

They inspected the en suite, where Rob tapped on the glass and checked the screws on the shower screen.

'There are five toilets in the house,' said Claudia.

'That's more loos than bedrooms. How many loos do people need?' asked Lisa.

'The fifth toilet is for guests. It's what people expect nowadays.'

They wandered into a room with a large screen where they heard someone ask a real estate agent if the projector came with the movie room.

'Imagine,' whispered Lisa, 'spending millions of dollars on the house and quibbling about whether the projector is thrown in.'

'That's how people get rich,' replied Claudia, 'by driving bargains and watching every cent.'

'How many agents have they got showing people around, anyway? There seems to be one in every room.'

'Several, but they only accompany the people who they think are serious buyers.'

'Which counts us out.'

They walked into a bedroom with pink mohair rugs draped over white doona covers. Lisa moved quickly to one side as two little girls pushed past, leaped onto the beds and threw cushions at each other.

'I think they belong to the bogan couple I saw downstairs,' muttered Claudia, leading Lisa and Rob out to the concrete balcony that encircled the house. 'They've come to see how the other half live.'

Including people like you, thought Lisa, and swallowed her words. Ever since they'd moved into Claudia's apartment, a memory had been running through her mind: an old woman shuffling by the school fence, calling out to them that she was hungry. Lisa had passed her lunch money through a gap in the fence. Claudia said the woman didn't deserve anything because she hadn't saved for her old age. Lisa had retorted that even if people worked hard, they might not have enough to live on later. They'd argued fiercely, until Belinda pointed out that no one was going to win and she wanted to sneak out to buy fish and chips.

Lisa bit her lip at the memory, realising at last that it was one of the reasons why she'd drifted apart from Claudia and Belinda since leaving school. On the rare occasions when they'd met as adults, only scraps from the past bound them together – giggling through chapel, tripping over each other's sticks at hockey practice, and yielding secrets to each other turn by turn, as they huddled on rainy days between the giant folds of a Moreton Bay fig tree near the school oval. Over the years, the demands of farm, family and work had engulfed them and they'd stopped meeting. Occasionally Belinda and Lisa emailed each other. At Christmas they both received the same typed letter from Claudia listing her achievements. Brag cards, Rob called them.

Lisa wondered why Claudia was bothering with her now: perhaps she was so busy working as a financial adviser she didn't have time for friends.

Walking into an alcove furnished with large pots containing spiky grasses and magazines fanned across a table, Lisa couldn't hold back her contempt for the house. 'Plenty of pot plants but not a book in sight.'

'Nowadays most people keep books in their study,' replied Claudia.

Lisa shrugged and walked downstairs to the backyard, where a row of Mongolian pear trees struggled to hide the neighbouring red-brick house.

When Claudia followed her and talked about how compact the

garden was, Lisa replied in a brittle voice, 'It's too bare. They need some hanging pots.'

'It's all clean lines nowadays – no clutter or junk like hanging flower baskets.'

'Or books, apparently.'

'Jeez, I like the gas barbecue, and the pool,' said Rob, gazing at the expanse of water shimmering over blue tiles.

'There's no room for anything else in the backyard,' said Lisa.

'There's a gazebo,' Claudia pointed out.

She flashed a smile, an odd bright smile, Lisa thought.

'Too much fancy wrought iron. And that bloody peacock on the top is ridiculous.'

'I like the peacock,' said Rob.

'The gazebo's too small.'

'What do you want, Lisa?' asked Claudia, an edge of sarcasm creeping into her voice. 'A bandstand like the one in the park?'

'No, more like a small rotunda where you can sit on a wooden bench and do a crossword.'

'I can't do them any more,' said Rob, walking into the gazebo, where he sat down and put his head in his hands.

Lisa followed him and they sat together while Claudia stood near the pool and talked on her mobile phone.

Glancing across at Rob, Lisa saw tears in his eyes. As she took his hand, an idea began to slowly form in her mind, unexpected and daring: a way to give Rob back as much of his old life as she could. He was worn down by strangers and specialists who asked him to count back by sevens from a hundred, quizzed him about the date and were puzzled when he joked that the last day he remembered clearly was the ides of March. He needed to spend time with people who knew him. He needed to walk and ride in open spaces. She'd noticed there were stables to rent at the edge of the park. If she bought the house, Rob could go riding there, and there'd be plenty of room in the house for family and friends to stay. She loathed everything about it but she would learn to live in it – for Rob's sake.

As they walked back to survey the front garden, she kept quiet about her resolution and talked to the real estate agent in a voice that sounded casual and non-committal. 'How do you mange to keep the lawn green with all the water restrictions?'

'We've got a new-property exemption. We're allowed to water every day.'

'You'd need a few tanks to keep this lot going. Good thing there's plenty of run-off from the roof.'

'That's right. Talking about water, Rob, can you please top up Almond's bowl.'

As Rob walked away, Lisa asked the agent how much he thought the house would sell for.

'We're hoping it might reach the two million dollar mark, even with the global recession,' he replied. He adjusted his tie as he considered the question. 'It's a magnificent house and people around here hold their properties tightly. I think we'll have a lot of serious bidders at the auction.'

'I'll outbid them.'

Claudia's eyes rounded with seeming disbelief. 'You can barely scrape up the money for the medical expenses, you told me the other day.'

'I could sell the water, not just on the farm but on our interstate properties as well. Rob's put everything in my name.'

'But there's no water to sell. There hasn't been rain there for years.'

'The government doesn't buy the water – they buy the rights to water.'

'Rob's family has farmed for generations.'

'Who's left now? He's an only child and we've no kids.'

'But you can't sell the water rights when you know that Rob wouldn't want you to sell them. It's taking advantage of his illness.'

'His illness is the reason I want to sell. If we bought this house, he could walk and ride in the park.'

'You don't know how to bid at an auction.'

'There's quite an art to it,' warned the real estate agent.

'Give me the forms and I'll register. Then we'll see if I can do it.'

After the auction, she rang Belinda to tell her she'd bought the house.

There was a pause at the end of the line.

'What is it? Is something wrong?'

'Claudia sucked you in.'

'Sucked me in?'

'She was probably in cahoots with the real estate agent. She boasts about her network of business friends, how they share clients. She'll get a commission from that property, I'm sure of it.'

'It wasn't like that. She took us to the house for a bit of fun, before we went on to serious house hunting.'

'She showed you the house because it was across the road from that park you like so much. That's what she does – she finds out what people want and works on their weak spots, their flaws. She boasted to me about it once.'

'So what are my flaws?'

'Pride, protectiveness towards Rob, and, sorry to say it, your pigheadedness. You'd better go back and have a look at the house. Make sure it's what you want.'

'It's too late. I've signed the papers.'

'There's ways around that. But if Rob likes it, go ahead – if you can stand Claudia winning.'

'Are we going to live in this house?' asked Rob.

'Yes,' replied Lisa, closing the front door.

'Could Ricky live here too?'

'Yes, once we've settled in. We'll bring him down in the horse float. But he can't stay inside, even though it'd be fun seeing piles of manure on those white tiles.'

'Where will we put him?'

'In the stable near the park. You'll be able to ride him every day.'

'I've always dreamt of riding in a big park,' said Rob, placing an arm around her waist. 'Let's waltz down the driveway. Come on, Almond, you can run ahead and help us keep time.' He twirled Lisa around then stopped. 'We'll live here, won't we?'

'Yes, we'll live here,' she laughed, trying to keep in step with him as he spun her around again. 'If that makes you happy – despite everything.'

He stopped dancing. 'What? Don't you like the house?'

'It has a few flaws,' she said. 'But we'll work on them. We'll be happy here.'

She picked up his hand, waited for him to take the lead and soon they were dancing across the lawn.